Bouquet of Traps

Also by Mary Pomfret and published by Ginninderra Press
Writing in Virginia's Shadow
Cleaning Out the Closet
The Hard Seed
Rain and Shelter (Pocket Poets)
Fractures (Picaro Poets)

Mary Pomfret

Bouquet of Traps

Love and loss are at the heart of *Bouquet of Traps*. A couple grieve for the tragic loss of their teenage son. A widower struggles to adjust to life without his wife. A house rebukes the love that drives its owner to shape it into something new. To love is human but the risks inherent in its allure can be akin to the fate of the fly attracted to the Venus fly trap. Theses sixteen vignettes explore many versions of love and its traps. The accompanying illustrations present visual responses to each micro story – a path through a forest; a fissure; a closed trap; barbed wire fashioned into a seemingly broken cross.

Deb Stewart

Mary Pomfret's first lines invite the reader into disconcertingly dark places, where characters lose their balance and where everything seems beyond repair and even the foxes deal. Stories flash past, made poignant by Julie Andrews's quiet monochrome sketches. Pay attention, because just when you think you recognise the phantoms from the past, looming just off the page, Pomfret will jerk you around and they'll stride back on, breaking up the picture. Characters become diffident, subside into despair yet hold onto, rather than harden against, hope. The writing is assured, offers a fierce kind of asceticism. We are never in any doubt that the narrator is in control. *Bouquet of Traps* unsettles but also satisfies.

Gay Lynch

Bouquet of Traps
ISBN 978 1 76109 123 0
Copyright © text Mary Pomfret 2021
Copyright © cover image and artwork Julie Andrews 2021

First published 2021 by
GINNINDERRA PRESS
PO Box 3461 Port Adelaide 5015
www.ginninderrapress.com.au

Contents

The web of our life is of a mingled yarn, good and ill together…
William Shakespeare

Fox Love

So, here's the deal, Vixen said. I am offering you my amber love. Can you see it glowing in my cupp'd hands, quivering just for you? See how it pulses and glows, a bright thing, a living thing, just for you.

Reynard scratched his head and looked mystified. Says he, Should I trust you, Vixen dear? I fear I am not sure and I am wary of your flattery. I can offer you my loving touch to warm your winter nights. I can offer you soft whispers to soothe your sorrowful soul. But of love's wily ways I know nothing. So, dear heart, what shall I do with your sweet offering?

So here's the deal, Vixen said. You have until morning's first light to accept or nay, because my dear one, this throbbing flame will suffocate at dawn if you deny destiny's kind bid.

Reynard scratched his head and looked perplexed. Says he, I fear you entice me with your sly seductive words and I must use my craft to fend you off. I can offer you a night embrace and a midnight kiss. But of love's wily ways I know nothing. So dear heart, what am I to do with your sweet offering?

So here's the deal, Vixen said. Accept my love or nay, but be quick for I have not time to waste. Everyone knows, but you may not, overtures left too long untended return to the beggar's heart. And I must point out, my dear one, that to turn one's tail on love's kind scent is foolishness most strange.

Reynard scratched his head and looked dismayed. Says he, Vixen, you try to trap me with your cunning words. You must know that you and I, we are the same. We must be free to trail and roam the grassy plains, the forests deep. I can offer you my wounded heart, my hunting breath, my dreaming soul. But of love's wily ways I know nothing. So dear heart, what am to do with your sweet offering?

So the deal is sealed, Vixen said. I will teach you all you need to know about the wily ways of love. I will stroke your chest and you will see that free spirits need love, even if they sleep and hunt alone.

Reynard scratched his head and smiled a crooked smile. Says he, The deal is never sealed.

A bouquet: an arrangement generally meant to please the receiver. A creative demonstration or gesture with symbolic meaning. Depending on the circumstances, a bouquet is a universal token of both mystery and gravitas, and often a gift of love. A wreath is another thing altogether.

Baby, Please Don't Go

Outer suburbs. Winter's morning. Early. She plunges her arms into the hot dishwater. Bubbles dance and burst around her elbows.

From behind, he says, There's no hope for us. It's over. It's done.

Front door slams. She grips the edge of the kitchen bench. Sobbing.

Seconds or minutes tick by.

She rushes to the door. He'd changed his mind. He'd be standing at the front gate. Waiting. She flings the door open. She would beg.

No. Gone.

Last time he left near shattered her.

Alone.

She looks inside the cracked brown tea caddy. Twenty-five cents left till the end of the week. Cigarettes. On the bench? Surely he didn't. But he did. He took the last packet.

Yes.

She stares out the grease-stained net curtains and pulls the thick green cardigan tight around her, tight. Shivering.

Heavy, her back to the wall, she sinks to the floor onto the cold tiles. The full bottle of sedatives in the wardrobe would do it.

No reason to go on. No reason at all.

A shrill demanding howl broke the stiff silence.

Piercing.

Demanding.

Hungry.

Familiar.

How could she have forgotten?

Her baby's first cry for the day.

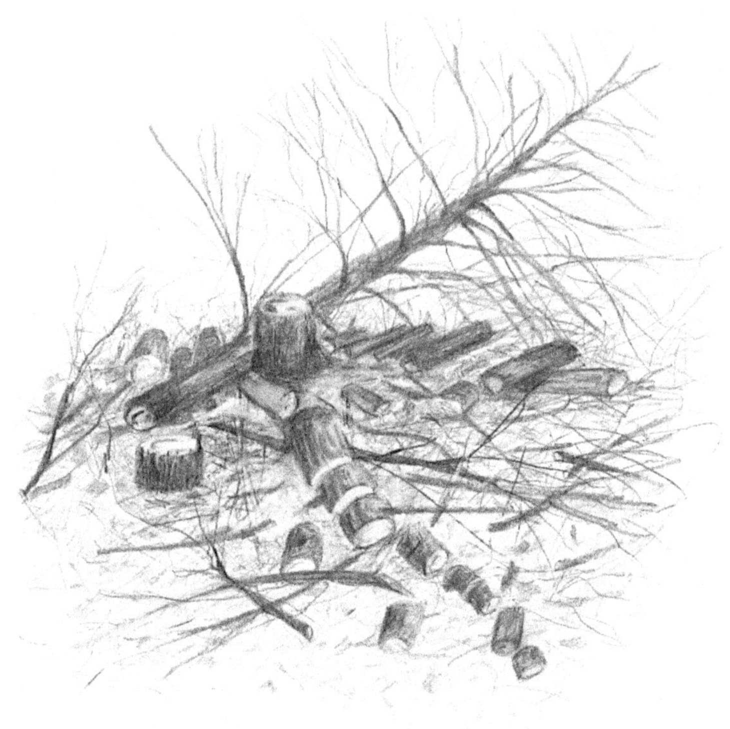

A Winter Lease

On New Year's Eve, I visited the house you moved to after you left me. You'd been gone for three months. You invited me and I went partly out of curiosity, but mainly because I didn't want to be alone on the last night of the year. I drove in the driveway and you came out to meet me, smiling. It was a good start, at least. But I could smell the stale carpet from the porch. You held the door open for me and I stepped inside. It was late afternoon and still hot and the heat of the house made the carpet smell more pungent, like cat's wee. I surveyed your lounge room as if I was standing in front of a stage set for a play that was about to start, a performance in which I did not have a role, not even as an understudy.

You'd placed your books in the bookshelf so neatly, with obvious care. Your record collection was piled high on the dark wooden floorboards speckled with cream paint. The landlord must have been in a hurry. Perhaps the previous tenant had punched a hole in the wall or a child had drawn a picture of a little dog with a black pen and he needed to cover it up quickly for you, the new tenant. Framed photographs adorned the high mantelpiece over the empty fireplace – pictures of your dead mother, your dead father, your dead sister, your dead brother. Our son, as a little boy, smiled down at me from his school portrait – grade three or four maybe. Twenty-seven now, he was well and truly alive. An unframed photograph of you and me from about twenty years ago was strategically placed in the centre of the display. How easily it could have placed face down, if you were expecting a visitor – a lady of the night maybe.

Sit down, you said. Make yourself at home. But it was never going to be my home: it was your home. I left well before midnight. You insisted that I did. You said you didn't want me driving home in the dark. I said that I had driven home many times before in the dark. But it is New Year's Eve, you said, and opened the front door for me to walk through. It was only nine o'clock and the fireworks didn't start till midnight.

You called and said you thought that it would be 'nice for us to get back together at some stage'. But you didn't say exactly when. You didn't give me a day, a month or a year. But one day, you said. You told me you'd bought a new chainsaw to help me cut down my dying pine tree. It would give me space in my garden for a new flower bed – irises and daffodils would work well, you said. They would bloom in the spring. In the heat of the day, you sawed away and the branches cracked and fell, one by one, to the ground. You said that I was better off without the dead tree, and that you would take all the branches and the pine cones away to save me the bother.

A few days later, the postman delivered a letter addressed to you. Thinking it best, I drove to your house and put it in your rusted letter box that was nailed loosely to a rotting timber post. I stood for a moment and glanced down the length of your driveway at the pile of neatly stacked wood at the side of your shed. You saw me and came to the gate.

So you're all set for winter, I said.

Guess so, you replied.

Common traps:

– Love, pure and simple (but, as we all know, there is no such thing)

– Love in the mist, especially in July

– Love in the dark night when the moon is behind thin clouds

– Love in the distance on the far horizon of hopes of heroes and heroines

– Love in the deep blue ocean of dreams and other discontents

Counting Cars

Lately, in the early velvet silence of Sunday mornings, I find myself counting cars, in my head. One. Two. The three a.m. cars are loudest – noisy mufflers – possibly P-platers looking for the last party, doing skids, giving up, going home. And I fall back into the haze of a dream and, usually, another loud muffler wakes me around four a.m. Dreadful. I understand this word now.

Five. Six. Full of dread. My father, when he was dying of tar-black cancer, told me he would wake every morning at this hour. The death hour, he called it; but strangely enough, he passed away one balmy afternoon, just after midday, in the golden autumn glow.

Fifteen… Seventeen… Twenty-eight.

For some reason, my counting, a rosary penance of a kind, echoes loudest when I am in the bathroom getting ready for the long day ahead. Perhaps it's the stark gloss of white tiles; the clinical smell of disinfectant; the cold stainless-steel taps – a reminder of hospital wards and mortuaries that summon death's cruel recall.

Thirty-three.

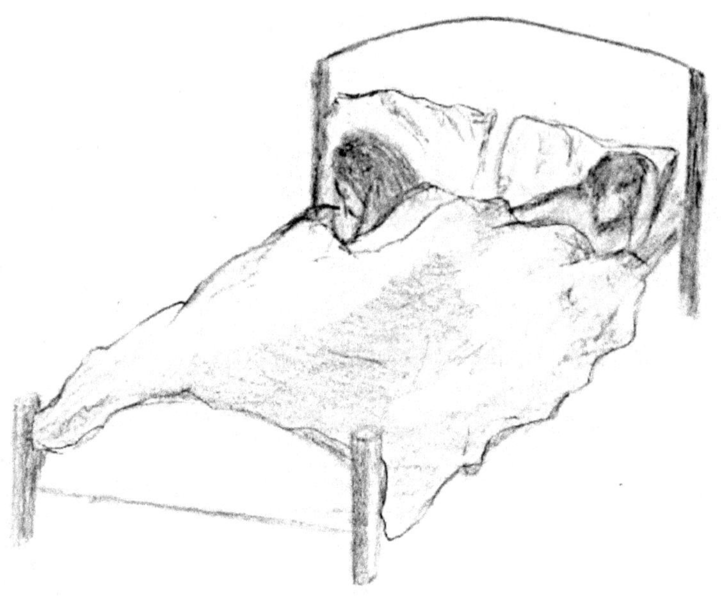

Ghost Pain

Light shone through the crack in the hotel room drapes. Jack reached across the cold expanse of white sheet that separated him from his wife of twenty-five years.

'I think I'll go for a walk along the beach,' Liz said, getting out of her side of the bed.

Jack wasn't going for a walk. He was waiting for his bacon and eggs to arrive. Liz pulled on her tracksuit and strolled down to the beach. Deserted. High tide. She'd read once that when you were wedged somewhere between an ending and a beginning, in a liminal space, you should sit under doorways, near thresholds, to tempt in the new. Today, she'd settle for just sitting on a park bench and staring out to sea.

When she returned, Jack asked if she'd had a good walk. But there's a big difference between asking a question and wanting to know the answer.

'What time does this wedding start?' Jack asked. It was the reason for their weekend away, wasn't it? 'Did you pack my blue tie?'

Jack spent most of the evening holding up the bar, chatting with the bridesmaid, Charlene, short and round in her frothy apricot dress. It was a rare thing now for Liz and Jack to go out anywhere together as a couple. The last time was when Liz had taken him to the English Department's Christmas break-up party.

Jack's only comment after the party had been, 'How long have people been calling you Elizabeth, Liz?' It was as if their love lay in a coffin like a dead thing, and they sat on either side, grieving its departure, invisible, silent. After they'd lost Jimmy, Liz had turned to literature and study, but just where Jack found solace, Liz wasn't sure.

Luckily, they didn't have too far to walk back to the hotel after the wedding. Jack stumbled rather than walked. He slept all night with his suit and shoes still on.

'Didn't Charlene look lovely last night?' were Jack's first words when he woke.

'Oh yes, indeed. Just like an apricot tart.'

'Don't be spiteful, Liz. It doesn't suit you. Or, at least, it never used to suit you. You know, I think I liked you better when you used to be you.'

Yes, it had been a slow thing, a tough thing, this change, this hardening between them.

Jack lay back on the bed and flicked on the television. He wouldn't even notice she was gone.

This time, when she reached the beach, the tide was out. Seagulls squawked above. Liz sat, again, on the same park bench. A dangerous game this hoping. A cold wind slapped her face. She moved forward on the bench, ready to stand, ready to go. But something, a lingering sense of a presence next to her, the familiar weight of an arm around her shoulders, a faint whispering breath in her ear, kept her there, sitting alone, staring out and longing for what was gone.

Advice for the unwary:

– Do not look for a reason

– Be sure to struggle, especially if told not to

– Hope for the best

– Avoid traps

Verification

It was white chocolate, definitely white, of that I am sure. The painting my father had brought to the art dealer's house was a watercolour. This man was an expert. He was going tell my father if it was a Turner or not. If it was a Turner, the art dealer would buy it, and my father could pay all the bills that were piling up, unopened behind the clock on our mantelpiece. My father had taken me along for company, hadn't he?

The house was big and dark and smelled the same as the chocolate. The chocolate had that musty smell, as though it had been opened and left sitting untouched in its wrapper for too long. It was broken into uneven pieces with edges ragged and sharp. He offered it to me on a plate, a white plate, chipped, I think. His hands were the hands of an old man, the backs of them shiny and speckled with brown spots. His fingers were bent and wrinkly, fingernails yellow and long. Needed cutting. Mum always cut my fingernails. Usually in the bath.

Would you like a piece? Yes, please – trying so hard to be good. Trying so hard to be polite and thinking of Mum cutting my fingernails in the bath. Leave the little girl with men for a while, he said. Leave her with me.

My father's back was stiff as he walked away, down the hallway, out the front door. The chocolate was hard and stale. It tasted like it smelled – musty. The man's breath was sour and his hands were dry and hard. Did I like school? Yes. Was I good girl? Yes? Could I keep a secret?

Where did my father go? Did he sit in the car and smoke Capstan unfiltered cigarettes? Did he bite his nails? Or did he read the paper and drink a cup of tea from a polystyrene cup?

On the way home, my father stopped at a garage and bought me an album for cards with pictures of butterflies, or was it free with the petrol? I was sent to bed early that night. I collected the butterfly cards for years after that. My mother was pleased the man had bought the painting. It was definitely white chocolate. White chocolate, on a plate.

A trap: a cruel deceit constructed to entice or ensnare the unwary wanderer. Traps are often disguised as something they are not. Traps are sometimes tricks presented as a possibility of escape only to lead to further enclosure or entrapment.

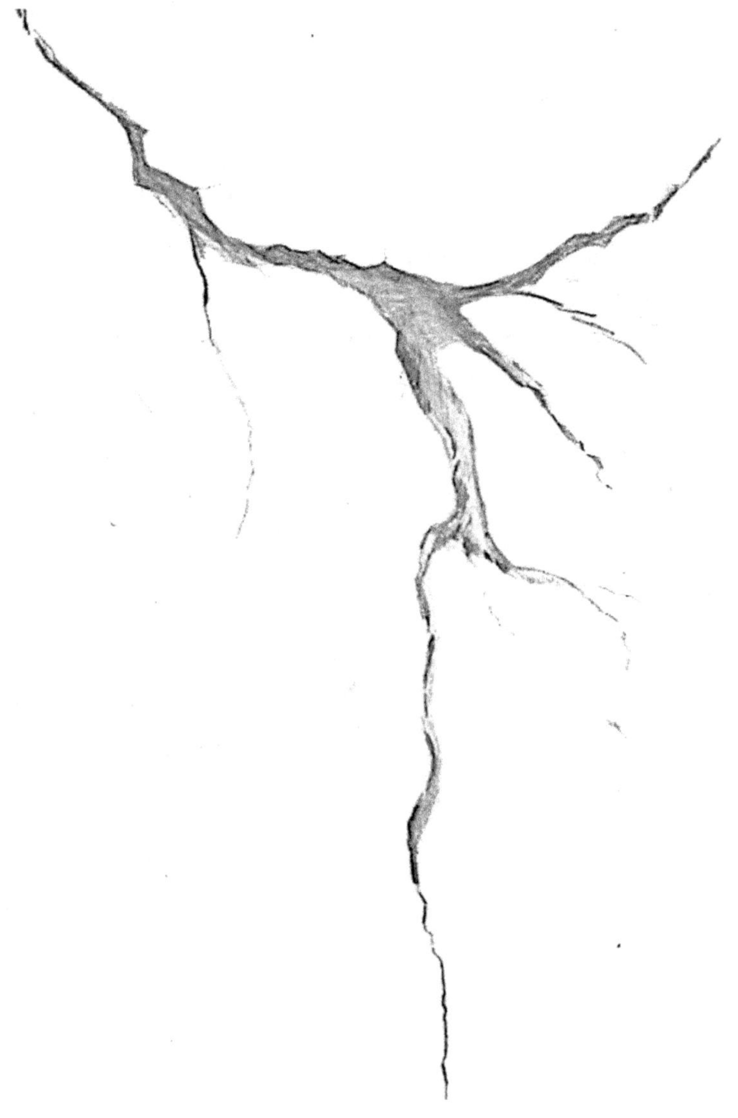

Saturday Night in the Gully

Saturday night hot and dark, lonely widow sits outside under rusty eaves looking out across roof lines uneven, front lawns parched, doors open wide to let in the air.

Saturday night long and black, lonely widow weeps drinking red wine, turned sour, to stave off memories of better days that weren't really better.

Saturday night he only hurt her where it wouldn't show, heavy doors always closed so no one heard. Only his rope in a shed brought her relief when he finally hung it from the beam.

Saturday night humid and still, lonely widow listens, nothing disturbs the quiet, except for the occasional howling dog, till, from across the valley of melting bitumen, voices crack into the thick night punching gaps in the air like holes in a wall.

Saturday night, baby cries, child screams, Dad don't. Woman yells, Get out. Gunna call the cops. Something drops, something stops. Car door slams. Rubber burns. Saturday night and someone is gone.

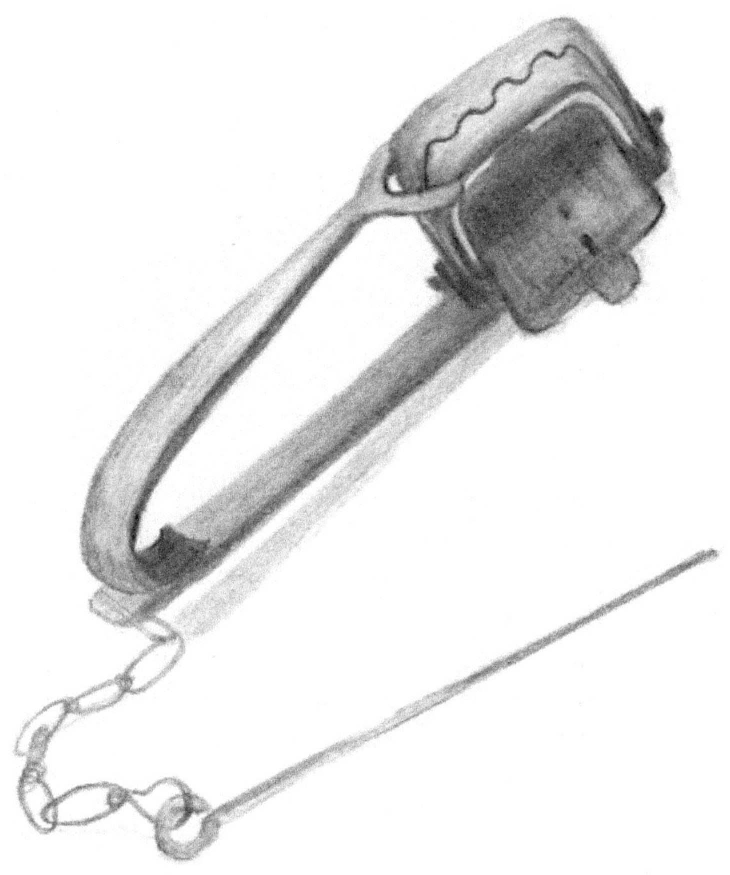

Nature Studies

Father used to like to set traps. Heavy metal traps to catch possums, Tasmanian devils and any other sort of wildlife he could skin and whose hides he could display as curiosities. Sometimes he would even kill snakes for their teeth. Snake's teeth make pretty necklaces, he told me once.

Brother and I would have to go with him at night when he checked the traps. We lived where the rainforest was thick and dark. Often, the animals would still be alive in the traps, squealing in agony, their paws hanging by bone and sinew. He would shoot the tortured things, toss them into a sack that he carried over his shoulder, and then, with brother and me trailing behind him, he would go back to our house and skin them on our back veranda. Once, and only once, he used a string net trap because he said it was more humane.

Mother made me a muff from a possum skin. When I wore the muff to Sunday Mass, I used to imagine I was a princess riding in a glass horse-drawn carriage, not the raggedy-looking skinny girl I must have been, walking down a dirt road with brother behind me and Mother in front pushing a newborn baby in a shiny black pram. My father never came with us to Mass.

Absent Wives

The first time a Frenchman opened his wallet and showed me a photograph of his wife, I was barely eighteen, and on a bus negotiating the unmade surface of a road in the desert.

Elle est ma mère, my fellow traveller said.

Your wife is your mother? I asked him.

Oui, he nodded. He was young like I was and later he kissed me in the night, forgetting his wife for a while.

The second time a Frenchman opened his wallet and showed me a picture of his wife, I was much older. He was a customer seeking my help with the purchase of a dining room table. I dutifully measured the table and gave him my sales pitch as to why this was the best table for him, the best table by far.

The table is only for me, he said.

Oh, well, it is only small, I lied. Not really all that big. Just a nice size for one.

This Frenchman was not young. He placed his hand on his chest. My wife was killed in a car accident – she was alone in the car. She is my heart, he said. We had had a family meal the night before – roast lamb with lots of garlic, he said.

He wanted a new table now because he couldn't bear to sit alone at the old one with without her, without his dear heart, his only love.

My sad wish is that I could see her just once more, he said.

I smiled my best salesperson's smile and I told him I couldn't help him with that.

'But the table will be just perfect for you,' I said as I took his cash and counted it.

Do Not Resuscitate

So who do you think you are coming here and rearranging me, making a heroine of yourself by rescuing me from what you perceived as my decline? Don't you know that I was quite happy as I was, with my blocked drains and broken windows? And you had the audacity to knock down my walls that I have spent years holding up, to pull up my boards and then, worst insult of all, to jack me up while you came underneath me in my all my dark and secret places. You wanted to 'strengthen my foundations', as your treacherous builder put it. Do you think I cared that I was sinking? I liked sinking. I wanted to sink. It was my natural destiny before you came and interfered. You couldn't leave well enough alone, could you? Now, thanks to you, I have to try and stand erect for another hundred years or more. Did it never occur to you for one moment that I might have been weary of being on top of this hill, in the wind and the rain and in the summer the scorching heat? Did you never think when you were slapping that glossy paint all over me, that I may have weathered enough storms? I didn't want to be sanded back, patched up, nailed and knocked back into shape just so you could be proud of me. I didn't want anyone to be proud of me. I just wanted to be left alone, on windy nights to rattle and shake, to sing my song of the past, to fade and disappear into the earth on which I stand. I had done my time but you gave a kiss of life. And I am not grateful.

Tunnel Vision

If I had known for one minute that the piano was going to fall on your head the way that it did, I would not had said the things that I did, and I would never have let the cat out of the bag, because how was I to know that the ocean would sweep your house to the sea one stormy night? And if I did, I would never have called you all those names (especially… Well, never mind) but you have to understand that such catastrophic events can never really be accurately predicted, no matter how clear the view through the crystal ball and when you drew the two of cups from the Tarot deck, I didn't for one minute imagine that you would leave and marry Bob (of all people, did it have to be Bob?) with his two tails and who sings like an owl and had I known that your heart would crack and splinter like pieces of a broken mirror, when the final curtain came down, I would have given you a book to read, a hand to hold to soothe your pain, I would have given you comfort of a kind and I would have told you, as gently as I could that, in fact, the future was yours in a box, with your name clearly spelled, and no matter how much you wished, you would not be able to return it to sender because some things are non-refundable and non-negotiable, but surely you must know that by now, after all you have seen, and all places you have been, and when you look into my eyes and I look into yours, it's like looking down a tunnel into the eyes of your mother and then her mother before her like an endless past, and if I look away all I can see is what can never be known.

Monday

Five forty-five a.m. A fine-boned woman in a wheelchair says, 'I often dance in my head.'

She dreams she closes her eyes and watches herself swirling and tripping the floor in her silver shoes, her toenails painted red as they once had been.

She dances with a cliché, a man tall dark and handsome. They dance to the slow strains of 'The Tennessee Waltz'.

Then the woman opens her eyes and says to me, 'I enjoyed that dance.'

'Are you a phantom?' I say to the outline of her shape as it fades into nothingness and I step out of her dream into my own.

The man I am dancing with is less of a cliché. His hands are hard like clay, his hair is the colour of sandstone and when he smiles he looks like a fox.

I wake to the heat of his breath and the warmth of his chest.

New Moon Homecoming

It was around midnight when the taxi pulled up outside my house. For a moment, I thought my family had put hundreds of sparklers in my garden to welcome me. I should have known better. When the taxi drove away into the night, I realised it was only my migraine aura, flashing zigzag lights, lightning-like, disturbing my vision and warning me that a headache could be on the way.

I went straight to my bedroom, fell down on my bed, grabbed the medication from my bag, put the tablets inside my cheek and waited for it to pass. Fifteen minutes was usually how long it lasted. I could just see the time on my clock – 12.02 a.m. I took deep breaths and at 12.18 the lights had gone and I could see clearly again. Slowly I got up from my bed. No headache this time.

I switched on the bedside lamp and looked around. I was home. It smelt the same. Frankincense and lavender. Nothing had changed. My house was just as I had had left it. Well, almost. Nothing can stay absolutely the same. I ran my fingers across my writing desk – just the thinnest layer of dust. Rose petals from the red bloom I had left in a crystal vase had dried out and fallen into a little stiff pile of faded hearts. A dead cockroach lay legs up on the kitchen bench.

I pulled open my thick floral curtains and looked out at the full moon shining through the gum trees. I don't recall ever seeing a moon in Asia. But just because I hadn't seen it, doesn't mean it wasn't there.

Version of Love

It was one of those days, you know, one of those shut-down days, those grey, wizened, chilly wind, no birds singing days. In front of me, along the path, two telegraph poles away, a man, middle-aged at least, stopped dead in his stride, turned and hugged the slim hooded figure next to him. Radiant heat from the hug warmed me, fleetingly. Second wife. Would have to be the second wife. Ten years younger than him. I'll just bet she is.

Closer now, only one telegraph pole away. He must be fifty, maybe more. Baggy green cords ballooning in the wind, he holds the hug and kisses the loved one's head. The hood, silky-lined, slides down from a crop of silver hair. Not trophy wife after all. Getting closer. Could it be first wife? No, too old. Mother, maybe?

Upon them now. No. It's not second wife, first wife or mother. The kissed one, the hugged one, the loved one is a small, frail, silver-haired old man, walking frame resting on the kerb. Feeling strangely warmed, privileged even to have witnessed this version of love and to be re-minded that true love takes many forms, I continue my solitary walk back home.

Hot Summer Night

He slung his bag over his shoulder. Shadows of the twisted ironbarks laced his thin hungry body. Soon, he would have to find a place to shelter.

The late afternoon sun blazed on the horizon. A flock of screeching white cockatoos cracked the silence of the forest. He stopped dead for a moment. Something sparkled up at him through the ochre-coloured dirt. Down on his haunches, he scraped the cracked dry earth. Only a fucken bottle top buried in the dust. And he was no stranger to dust. Nothing good ever came to him. No hope.

A hot wind stirred his fine sandy hair. In the distance the sound of cars. Probably kids doing skids on the flat. Better walk the other way. Strangers. Best to stick to himself. Always. Turning, he walked on down the narrowing path into the thickness of the forest. Dry leaves and twigs snapped and crunched under his scuffed brown boots.

He reached into the pocket of his faded flannelette shirt. Shook the box. Plenty left. He always carried them close to his heart. Just about the only thing he could rely on. They'd never failed him – not so far, anyway. Redheads.

Death is a Song No One Wants to Sing

Raindrops glisten like tears in the late afternoon sun. Wipers scrape against the windscreen – left to right, right to left, left to right – on the long drive home, just as the sun is beginning to set.

'*Il pleut.*'

'Have you been watching foreign films again?' he says.

She glances sideways at his profile. No need to reply. He knows that she's been having French lessons, just for something different, something to take her mind off things. She hadn't really been speaking to him anyway. It just came out in French. Just thinking out loud.

The silence is broken only by the slapping of the wipers. It's pelting down now. They should have left earlier. But she had wanted to spend more time with him, with Jack. To pull out the weeds that had grown since last time. To arrange the flowers in a vase at the base of the headstone. White roses. To dust off the cold marble. To talk to him. To tuck him in.

To tell him how much she loved him, how much she missed him, how his cat had had kittens, how his friend had been accepted into medicine, how the girl across the road had become pregnant, how his grandmother had been in hospital but she was going to be okay…so many things. But there was never enough time…never.

'Time to go.'

That was the worst moment, when they had to leave. He took her by the arm. Pulled her up. Not quite roughly. He almost dragged her, but not quite, to the car and they drove slowly down the cemetery driveway. She turned her head and watched the grave until it was out of sight, completely gone. And then she waved, just as she always did, and the tears fell just as they always did.

'We shouldn't have stayed so long.'

She doesn't answer. Night begins to fold around them. It's raining so hard now that it's difficult to see the road. The headlights seem to come thick and fast. They'd moved from the country back to the city, thinking that it'd be better to start again somewhere else, to try and forget. New house, new job, new people. But on the last Sunday of the month they made the same trip, the trip they never could not make, the trip to see Jack.

Nearly three years now, three years since the knock on the door in the middle of the night. She'd been the one to answer it. The policeman and woman had both looked so young, standing in the doorway, the moon shining behind them. Funny how those things stick in your mind. A joyride gone wrong. Everything that could be done had been done. Nobody's fault. They were very sorry. Everyone was very sorry. Just sixteen years old.

She looks down at her watch. It wouldn't be much longer now. When they got home, they wouldn't speak. She would sit in Jack's room and cry until she went to bed. He would go out to the shed and drink until he couldn't remember anything, couldn't feel anything. In the morning, he would bring her in a cup of tea, kiss her cheek before he left for work and whisper, 'Have a good day.' And so they would begin again.

The traffic is heavy now they have hit in the city. She hugs her coat closer to her, pulls the fur collar around her neck. Finally, the car swings into their driveway and stops under the carport. He turns off the headlights. The house is dark. They walk towards the front door, stones crunching under their feet. She holds out the palm of her hand in the cold night air.

'Do you think it will it ever stop raining?

Acknowledgements

Earlier versions of these works have been published, exhibited and awarded as follows:

'Verification', *Hecate*, 2009, and *Cleaning Out the Closet*, Ginninderra Press, 2014

'Death is a Song No One Wants' (as 'The Visit'), *Idiom 23*, 2016, and *Taheke*, 2019

'Ghost Love', Co.lab Exhibition, 2018

'Hot Summer Night', featured in Byron Bay Writers' Festival Flash Fiction Competition, 2018

'A Winter Lease', Peter Cowan Short Story Award, 2018, and *Taheke*, 2019

'Nature Studies', *Taheke*, 2019

'New Moon Homecoming', *Mensicus*, 2020

About the Artist

Julie Andrews (1962, Melbourne) has a practice which encompasses both private studio work and public art. Andrews lives and works as an artist in Bendigo. She received her Bachelor of Visual Arts at Latrobe University, Bendigo, and completed a Master of Arts (Art in Public Space) with HD at RMIT, 2014. She has undertaken a number of large public and private commissions and has held over twenty solo exhibitions and contributed to thirty group shows in various locations throughout Australia. Further afield, she has undertaken residencies where she made and exhibited artwork for the SoHo Gallery, Singapore; the Shipley Gallery, Newcastle, England; and at '33 Bund' gallery, Shanghai. Her work is held in private collections in Australia and internationally in Newcastle and Sunderland, England; Banff, Scotland; South Korea; Singapore; and the USA.

List of illustrations